For my Mum and Dad with Love x

First published 2005 by Cornish Cove Publishing

This edition published 2005

This book has been typeset and designed by PH Media - 01726 891111

Printed by St Ives (Roche) Ltd. - 01726 892400

British Library Cataloguing in Publication Data
A catalogue record for this book is
available from the British Library.

ISBN 0-9550928-0-9

To the far south and very much to the west, where the sun sets last over a glistening ocean of every shade of green and blue, Sennen Cove looks out over Whitesands Bay of warmed Gulf-Stream waters which belong to the Atlantic.

ONE AND ALL

Bude

Tintagel

Launceston

NORTH

Padstow

Wadebridge

Bodmin

Liskeard

Newquay

St Austell

TRURO

Saltash

Plymouth

St Ives

Redruth

Hayle

Falmouth

St Just

Penzance

Helston

Sennen

Newlyn

Lands End

Isles of Scilly

Lizard Point

W

S

2

Sennen Cove

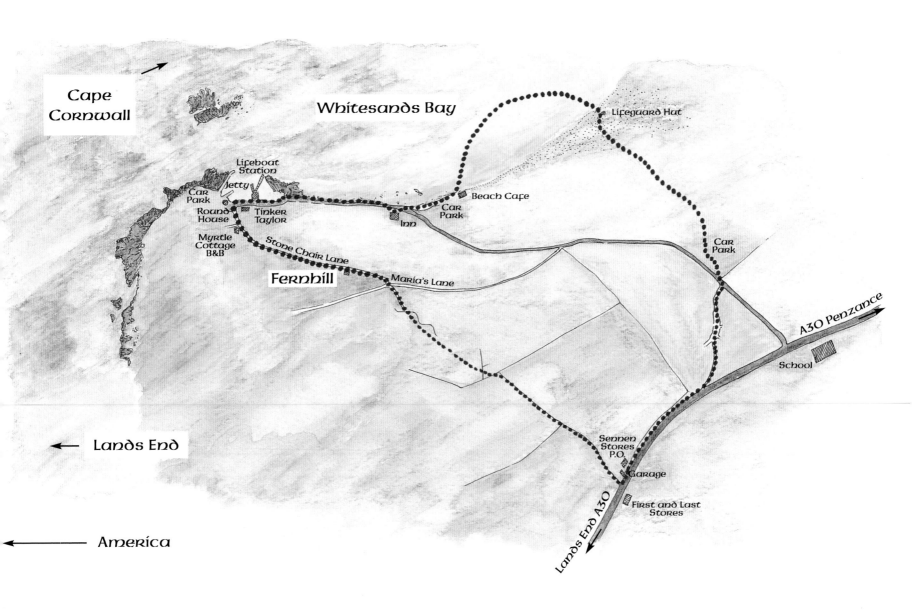

Cape Cornwall

Whitesands Bay

Lifeguard Hut

Lifeboat Station

Jetty

Car Park

Round House

Tinker Taylor

Beach Cafe

Car Park

Inn

Car Park

Myrtle Cottage B&B

Stone Chair Lane

Fernhill

Maria's Lane

A30 Penzance

School

Lands End

Sennen Stores P.O.

Garage

First and Last Stores

America

Lands End A30

Shanti's Trail

The house called *Fernhill* sits high on the cliff amongst lush wild ferns, a mere mile from rugged Lands End, overlooking Sennen's beautiful Cove and green-blue ocean. In the house live two occupants ~ an old man, who used to fish in the bay for his living, and his dog. Everyday they sit, each to their own armchair, side by side, at the large window that looks out over the bay. The old man stares through his large binoculars at all the sights to be seen in and around the ocean before him.

4

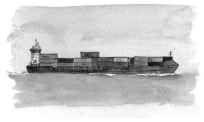

Small Sailing Boat   **Sennen Life Boat**   **Small Fishing Boat**   **Container Ship**

Many, many boats and ships of different kinds sail past each day. Some sail close to the shore, and some sail far out on the distant horizon.

Oil Tanker   **Vehicle Carrier**   **Passenger Ferry**   **Cruising Sailboat**

In a little book by the side of his arm chair, the old man lists all the different sea vessels that pass through the bay each day. Sometimes his binoculars are powerful enough for him to see even the name of a boat.

Beam Trawler   **Reefer**   **Tall Ship**   **Motor Yacht**

Herring Gull

Guillemot

Gannet

Many, many birds of all different kinds can be seen flying around the bay. Some fly inland, and some fly far out at sea. The old man loves to identify all the different types of birds, and he writes a log of all the ones that he spots each day. Sometimes, if there is a rare bird, or a new arrival to the shore, the old man makes a quick telephone call to the person at the local wildlife preservation society, to inform them what he has spotted, where, and the precise time of day that he spotted it.

Kittiwake

Cormorant

Chough

The old man loves to watch out for marine creatures that swim in the waters of Whitesands Bay. Sometimes he sees nothing, but occasionally, he spots a basking shark in the water, or some seals on the distant rocks. Most of all the old man loves to watch out for dolphins swimming in the bay. With his experience of watching the sea, the old man still can never predict when the dolphins will come. It is very special when the dolphins do come to swim and play in the bay. When the dolphins come, the old man remembers the happy times when his wife was with him, and they would both watch the dolphins in the waters below their home. At such times they would both feel very lucky to be living in the beautiful coastal village of Sennen, near Lands End.

So when the dolphins come into the bay, it is like having his wife back again by his side. The old man feels comforted as he fondly remembers the times they spent together, sitting in the window of their home, perched high on the cliff, above the cove, overlooking the bay.

7

Nowadays, Shanti occupies the armchair in which once sat the old man's wife. There is now a blanket on **his** chair, and a bone, and an old tennis ball, and a squeaky toy which squeaks from time to time, and a piece of old rope washed up from the sea. On the floor beside his chair, are three bowls. One is full of water. Another has a small amount of food in it that Shanti has left over from his breakfast. And the third bowl is empty.

Shanti enjoys sitting in the armchair beside the old man. Shanti enjoys watching him looking out to sea, fiddling with his binoculars and occasionally taking his pen to write something down in one of his little log books. Shanti feels it is a dog's duty to guard the little log books, because he instinctively knows that they are important to the old man. Shanti always feels very special to be sat in the window, in such a comfortable chair with nice things just for a dog.

Because of this, Shanti tries always to sit very upright and proud in his armchair, that is, until he becomes sleepy and decides to curl up instead and take a nap. The old man likes to take a nap each day too. So, when the birds and boats and marine creatures, and people on the beach, can no longer see two figures in the square bay window of the house, high up on the cliff above the cove, it is sure to be because both the old man and his dog are taking their daily nap.

Unlike most dogs, Shanti does not sleep for very long, and so when he awakes from his dreaming, he normally finds the old man still snoozing beside him, snoring gently, his large binoculars resting on the little log books on the small table.

As is usual for Shanti dog after his nap, he stands up in his armchair on all four paws and arches his back. Then he climbs down from the chair onto the rug, and takes a long stretch, this time putting his two front paws far in front of him and pushing his rear end up as high as he can, whilst looking up to the ceiling with his head.

Next, he slowly pads his way across the room, carefully placing each paw so as not to make too much noise with his claws.

Passing through the doorway, Shanti creeps down the wooden staircase which always creaks in the same place. At the bottom of the staircase, he walks through a doorway which leads into the workshop.

The old workshop houses lots of clutter, bric-a-brac, pieces of pottery, a kiln, and things from fishing days gone by. Shanti crosses the cool, gritty floor and approaches an old wooden door, where daylight shines through the cracks and joins in the wood that has been rotted by the damp sea air over many years.

Pushing up a rusty metal catch with
his nose allowing this door to open,
Shanti steps into the outside world
of the garden. As he sniffs the fresh sea air and listens to the
sounds of the ocean below, the rusty metal catch gently
clicks back into place, as the door closes behind him.

Being outside, alone and free to wander as he pleases, is what Shanti loves to do when he isn't sitting proudly by the old man in the upstairs window looking out to sea.

In his usual manner, Shanti wanders across the gravel and down onto the lawned area that is hedged thickly with different types of shrubs and bushes. Beyond the lawn sparkles the jade and turquoise waters of the distant bay. Between two Hydrangea bushes ~ one flowering pink and one flowering blue ~ is a gap large enough for Shanti to push his way through. Once through this gap in the hedge, he finds himself in Stone Chair Lane. On this occasion, Shanti walks up to the top of the lane, straight across Maria's Lane and on into Esther's Field, where he follows the footpath beside the thatched house that leads into the cow field.

Standing around in one far corner of the field, the cows munch at the grass. They do not notice Shanti as he trots over their grazing land whilst sniffing the country air. At the stone stile Shanti walks down the path on the right, and before long he is at the cattlegrid by the main road. Some cars speed past. The noise of the engines startle Shanti and he stops in his tracks.

He sits on his hind legs and gives himself a great big scratch of his left ear with his left hind paw. On the other side of the road a mother and child come out from the grocer's store. Shanti hears their voices and the giggling of the child. They cross the road and head for where Shanti now sits, motionless on the grassy edge of the path by the fence, that separates it from the crop-field.

The woman carries a shopping bag, out of which pokes a long stick of French bread. Walking on by, she and the child do not notice a dog attempting to take a bite out of the long stick of bread as it passes its nose. Shanti, being rather slow, manages only to get a few crust crumbs between his teeth.

One more scratch of his left ear and then Shanti begins moving again, turning immediately left where he finds himself in a busy place indeed.

There is a van and two people. They stand chatting as one fills the vehicle with petrol. They do not notice Shanti, as he strolls past on the other side from where they are standing. Barnie does notice Shanti however. Barnie is the dog who lives at The First & Last Filling Station, and he has spotted Shanti and stares hard at him from his resting place outside the entrance of the garage workshop. Another creature has also spotted Shanti. He is the old ginger and white tom cat called Oliver, who is sprawled out on the wall which runs in front of the Post Office next door. Oliver stares hard at Shanti. But Shanti just keeps looking straight ahead as he walks on.

15

Suddenly a nice smell catches Shanti's attention, so he sniffs the air and looks around in the direction that the smell is coming from. On the ground outside the entrance of the Post Office is a shopping bag, and next to this bag stands a woman. She is reading the adverts on the notice board outside the shop. The woman does not notice a dog creep up from behind. The woman does not hear her shopping bag rustle as a dog pokes its nose into it. On the other side of the door, inside the Post Office, Mac the Scottie has seen Shanti and is growling and jumping about frantically. The woman outside does not notice Mac inside. The woman does not notice as a dog strolls off down the road, with **her** large Cornish pasty poking out either side of its jaws.

Shanti trots on fast now with **his** pasty, along the pavement and down a side alley on the left. Here he lets go of the pasty from his jaws and places it on the ground in front of him. He then crouches down on all four legs, his belly resting on the ground, and eats the warm pasty.

Only a single crumb remains on the ground when Shanti gets up from his crouching position. He continues his journey across Mayon Green Crescent, a short way down the main Cove Road, and through a wide opening on the right that leads him into a large grassy area where cars are parked.

Shanti walks around some of the parked cars, unnoticed by the families who are laying out their picnics on blankets. Shanti can feel a breeze now and he can hear the familiar sound of the ocean. He sniffs the air, looks up, and sees the vision of the sparkling water stretching far into the distance. From this high point on the dunes, way above the beach below, Shanti feels a surge of excitement run through him as he is energised by the expansiveness of the glorious view that is all his.

19

He then bounces down the grassy sloping pathway, beside the large granite rocks, taking care not to step into the rabbit holes all around. As the pathway becomes steeper, Shanti uses his hind legs like brakes to stop him going faster than he wants. As the pathway becomes narrower, the long firm spiky grasses tickle Shanti's nose and body as he brushes past on his journey, down towards the sea.

The sea air smells fresher and fresher. The sound of the ocean ahead and the lapping waves, becomes louder and louder. As he paws his way down the wide wooden steps, Shanti soon feels his legs sinking into the soft warm sand of the beach itself. Way ahead of him, some people are standing on the decking of a wooden hut that is built into the grassy sand dunes. This is the lookout station for the Lifeguards, who are busy chatting and peering through large binoculars. None of the lifeguards spots a dog descend from the path, and then make its way down to the main part of the beach.

20

Meandering and sniffing his way across the sand, Shanti is startled by the sudden roar of an engine, as a beach quad-bike speeds down from the wooden hut, and sprays sand all around as it turns down towards the sea itself. Shanti shakes the sand from his fur and then walks on, following the tracks of the quad-bike which is now a long way off down the beach.

To the left and to the right the bright golden sand seems to go on forever, and the sparkling ocean glistens all around filling the gap between the sand and the sky. Shanti's eyes and ears are alerted to the sights and noises of beach life.
He has many sensations as he walks closer to the water's edge, feeling and smelling the dark seaweed beneath his paws, which interests him. The sound of the roaring waves overwhelms Shanti, and for a moment he feels anxious, alone and disorientated.

21

Standing, looking out at the vast seascape, Shanti is abruptly startled out of his gazing by the screaming and laughter of children playing around the granite rocks and pools. Clusters of people are lying, sitting, standing and playing all around him. Now anxious to be gone from the noise and atmosphere of the beach, Shanti makes his way across the sand in the direction of the sun, for he senses this is the way home. With his nose bowed low and his ears pressed tightly to his head, Shanti looks only just a short way ahead. He moves swiftly, avoiding the people and the rocks. The squawking sounds of the seagulls can be heard as they hop all around and swoop in the air.

Soon there are more and more people, more and more rocks, more and more noises, and the smell of suncream. A building comes into view. It is The Beach Cafe and Restaurant. Shanti simply goes where his legs take him, and before long he senses different people staring at him and hands beckoning him to come in a particular direction. Shanti looks up briefly and nervously as he feels human hands touching him on his back and patting him on his head and neck. He senses that these are kind, caring hands reaching out to touch him. Dog lovers' hands. Then amidst all this Shanti senses something harsher. Still the sound of a human voice but this time it is a sharp, *"Tut, tut..., dogs on the beach - it shouldn't be allowed!"*. Shanti does not understand, since the only words he knows are, *'good boy'*, *'breakfast'*, *'rope'*, *'cake'*, *'ball'* and *'tea'*, but he knows the voice is directed at him and sounds critical of his presence. Shanti immediately feels that he wants to be far away from the busy atmosphere of this place.

Shanti looks up and smells more interesting smells, and he sees a hand dangling some more nice smelling things in front of his nose. The sounds of warm human laughter make Shanti feel good, so he decides to sit and wait for more tit-bits to be offered.

Shanti quickly manoeuvres his way across the cove car park and straight over the main Cove Road, where a large truck screeches to a halt beside him. Paying no attention to this, Shanti soon finds himself in the grounds of the Old Success Inn, which sits at the foot of the fern-covered cliff.

From nowhere, something lands in Shanti's path just ahead of him. He sniffs it and it smells good and so he eats it. He hears voices and laughter and the clinking sounds of glasses and cutlery on plates.

His head is stroked and one of his front paws is taken and rubbed. Gently and gratefully Shanti accepts more nice smelling food. The words, *"No more. No more food doggy... where's your owner?"* are spoken.

Since no more nice smelling food is offered in his direction, Shanti gets back onto all four legs and proceeds in the direction of the promenade. The memory of the nice tasting food that he has just been fed lingers in Shanti's mind. He is content as he walks his usual route along the railings of the promenade, the green-blue ocean beside him, and a feeling of tiredness and a longing for his chair.

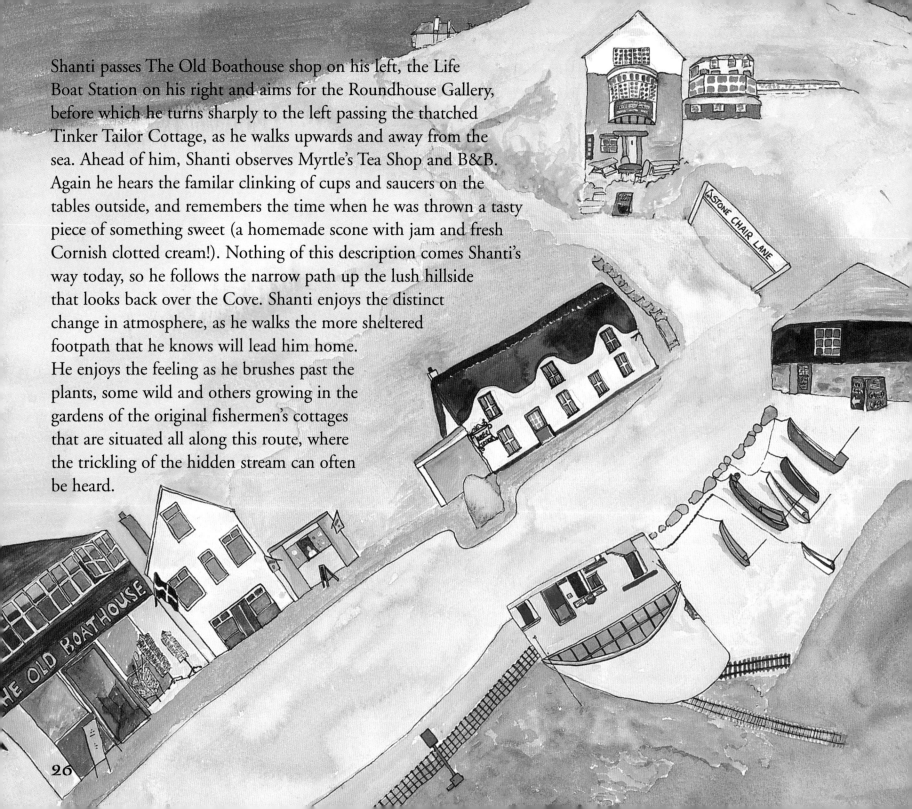

Shanti passes The Old Boathouse shop on his left, the Life Boat Station on his right and aims for the Roundhouse Gallery, before which he turns sharply to the left passing the thatched Tinker Tailor Cottage, as he walks upwards and away from the sea. Ahead of him, Shanti observes Myrtle's Tea Shop and B&B. Again he hears the familar clinking of cups and saucers on the tables outside, and remembers the time when he was thrown a tasty piece of something sweet (a homemade scone with jam and fresh Cornish clotted cream!). Nothing of this description comes Shanti's way today, so he follows the narrow path up the lush hillside that looks back over the Cove. Shanti enjoys the distinct change in atmosphere, as he walks the more sheltered footpath that he knows will lead him home. He enjoys the feeling as he brushes past the plants, some wild and others growing in the gardens of the original fishermen's cottages that are situated all along this route, where the trickling of the hidden stream can often be heard.

Monbretia

Wild Fern

Shanti does not know about Hydrangea bushes, except that he sometimes walks into a large bulbous flowerhead. Shanti cannot see the vivid orange colour of the very Cornish Monbretia growing profusely in every nook and cranny of this hillside, except that the long flowering stems often tickle his nose as he walks his journey home. Shanti enjoys brushing past the delicate flowers of the Fuchsia bushes, and feels comforted by the shapes of the green wild ferns which thrive all around.

Hydrangea

Fuschia

Walking for the five or so minutes along this pathway, Shanti notices how the sounds change. As the noises of the harbour fade into the distance, so the hum from the people on the beach and the ocean beyond become more distinct again. When he reaches the bench (where people can rest and take in the view), Shanti soon turns off right, to get back to his home, his chair and his favourite companion.

The two large granite pillars at the entrance of *Fernhill* come into Shanti's view. He walks along the driveway towards the vision of a house, his home. As is usual, on his return from his wanderings, Shanti's tail wags uncontrollably as his bright eyes look up at his window and the excitement of his homecoming is felt in his stomach.

On reaching the weathered wooden door of the workshop, Shanti raises himself on his hind legs. He uses both his front paws and his nose to push up the catch which opens the door, allowing him back inside. Soon Shanti is in the main house once again and creeping back up the stairs from whence he came.

At the top of the staircase, Shanti sees the now sun-filled room where the old man sleeps deeply in the armchair. He pads his way back across the room towards his dog bowls. Very soon Shanti is lapping at the water in the first bowl and finishing off the small amount of food in the second bowl. As if by magic, Shanti is soon curled up in his comfortable old chair, next to his friend, feeling safe and very tired. He breaths a big breath that sounds like a heavy sigh, closes his eyes and falls into a deep doggy sleep.

About twenty minutes later, Shanti hears the old man's familiar voice. *"Here's your tea Shanti boy"*. Shanti opens his eyes and raises his head slightly, and observes his companion bending down pouring tea into one of the empty bowls. *"Here's your tea, Shanti boy"*, repeats the old man, *"...wake up now, it's good for your fur, you ole sleepy dog you!"*.

Slowly, very slowly, because he is unsteady on his feet, the man sits back down in his old armchair. Beside him on the small table is a tea-pot, milk jug, cup and saucer, and a plate with a large fruit cake on it.

Shanti lifts his head further, sniffs the air, then stands up and arches his back into a stretch before climbing down off his chair and stretching again. He looks into the bowls on the floor beside his chair. Soon Shanti is drinking the warm milky tea that the old man has just poured out for him, and as he does so a whole piece of fruit cake lands in the middle bowl. Shanti gratefully eats and drinks from each bowl in turn.

The sound of the old man's voice is heard once again. *"There's a good boy Shanti. That tea it's good for your fur you know... so my mother used to say. Shanti boy, I wish I could take you out into the fresh air a bit. If only my legs would go like they used too. We'd go for good long walks, wouldn't we Shanti boy. Perhaps that's why you're not looking so slim of late".*

Shanti never exactly knows what the old man is trying to communicate, but the tone of his voice always makes Shanti feel loved and secure and happy to be a dog. The old man picks up his large binoculars and observes the magnificent view once again. The sun is still high in the sky and the ocean is still alive with boats and wildlife, for those that look close enough to see. The old man makes some more entries into his log books and his dog remains curled up in the chair for the rest of the afternoon, floating in and out of sleep. Shanti, the wandering dog of Sennen and the Lands End (if the old man but knew it!) feels completely relaxed and contented. He knows that he belongs.

"There's gonna be a glorious sun set tonight Shanti boy".